LITTLE LOST FOX CUB
The Cub's Adventure

Written by Louis Espinassous
Illustrated by Claudine Routiaux
English text by Patricia Lantier-Sampon

For a free color catalog describing Gareth Stevens' list of high-quality books, call 1-800-341-3569 (USA) or 1-800-461-9120 (Canada).

Library of Congress Cataloging-in-Publication Data
Espinassous, Louis.
  [Petit renard perdu. English]
  Little lost fox cub, on the trail of Little Fox / Louis Espinassous ; [illustrated by] Claudine Routiaux.
      p. cm.
  Title on added t.p., inverted: Little lost fox cub, the cub's adventure.
  Summary: Mother Fox searches for Little Fox, trailing him by his scent and the other clues he has left behind, which the reader is encouraged to find in the illustrations. Closing the book and turning it over produces the story of Little Fox's adventure.
  ISBN 0-8368-0927-0
  1. Foxes—Juvenile fiction. [1. Foxes—Fiction. 2. Picture puzzles.] I. Routiaux, Claudine, ill. II. Title. III. Title: Little lost fox cub, the cub's adventure.
PZ10.3.E723Li 1993
[E]—dc20   92-27116

North American edition first published in 1993 by

Gareth Stevens Publishing
1555 North RiverCenter Drive, Suite 201
Milwaukee, Wisconsin 53212, USA

Printed in the United States of America

1 2 3 4 5 6 7 8 9 97 96 95 94 93
Gareth Stevens Publishing
MILWAUKEE

Little Fox opens one eye as a butterfly lands softly on his nose. Very slowly, Little Fox gets up. His mother has forbidden him to move away from the spot during nap time. But Little Fox takes a few steps and follows the butterfly as it spins toward the forest.

Munch-crunch. . . . Crunch-munch.

Something is nibbling in the underbrush!
It's a family of field mice. Little Fox
prepares to pounce: too late! The mice
dive into their shelter. Nose in the air,
Little Fox jogs along the pathway to
the meadow.

TAP-tap-tap-tap. . . . TAP-tap-tap-tap!

Little Fox runs into a family of rabbits, but one bunny has already sounded an alert. A fireworks display of small white tails explodes in all directions as the bunnies hop quickly away.

Aaah! The scent of raspberries!
Little Fox dives into the thicket and treats
himself to the ripe berries. The delicious,
sugary juice runs down his chin.

THWACK! . . . THWACK!
Nearby, a deer butts a young birch tree.
The deer seems angry.
THWACK! . . . THWACK!

A shiver of fear travels down Little Fox's
spine. Where is the way back to
his mother?

Little Fox hesitantly starts down a small path.
He trots along, eager to find his mother.

GRRR. . . . GRRR. . . .
Little Fox is scared. A big fox, a stranger,
leaves its droppings nearby. The odor is
strong and terrible in Little Fox's nose.

"Mother! Mother!" cries Little Fox as he
gallops quickly away.

GROINK! GROINK!

Little Fox foolishly approaches a group of
wild boars. The mother boar chases him.
Little Fox runs away as fast as he can.

"Mother! Mother!"

Whoa! Whoa! Ruff! Ruff! MOOOO! MOOOO! Baaa! Baaa!

Strange noises, unfamiliar scents . . . Mother Fox had warned him not to wander onto human pathways. But Little Fox, without thinking, wildly crosses the path.

Yipe! Yipe! Yipe! As he scurries under the fence, he hooks a piece of his fur in the barbed wire.

QUACK!   QUACK!   CROAK!

What a strange place! Little Fox
has never been here before. He
does not recognize anything.
Lost! He is completely lost!

Exhausted, trembling, he pushes
through the thick reeds.
"Mother! Mother!"
He will never be able to find her.

But . . . Little Fox stretches his
snout under the grasses. He sniffs.
That scent, so sweet, so familiar . . .

"MOTHER!"

But how did Mother Fox find her little lost fox cub?
To find out, close the book and turn it over.

To find out, close the book and turn it over.

But how did Little Fox get lost?

"LITTLE FOX!"

LITTLE LOST FOX CUB
On the Trail of Little Fox

Written by Louis Espinassous
Illustrated by Claudine Routiaux
English text by Patricia Lantier-Sampon

On the trail . . . like a detective!
All of the animals encountered by the foxes leave
clues behind — on the ground, in the trees, and
on the rocks. These clues and Mother Fox's keen
sense of smell help her find her little lost fox.
You, too, can help Mother Fox in her search by
looking closely at the drawings and finding the
clues. And, after reading these stories, you can
be a detective in real life — by guessing which
animals have passed through the area around
your home by the clues they have left behind.

Gareth Stevens Publishing
MILWAUKEE

Mother Fox slowly awakens. She
opens one eye; she sniffs. . . .
The air is empty — empty of the
warm scent of her little fox.

Oh, no! He's gone!
With a single leap, she is on her feet.

Nose to the ground, Mother Fox searches. Near the wood, faint in the dead leaves, she finds the scent and the trail of Little Fox. But what was he doing near the oak tree? Where has he gone?

In the fine sand on the meadow, in the middle
of many footprints, run the tracks of Little Fox.
He must have frightened the other animals away!

Hmmm! The delicious smell of raspberries!
Little Fox must have had a wonderful time.

But Mother Fox suddenly discovers a tree that has
been disturbed. Her heart tightens. She sniffs the
ground and begins to run.

Mother Fox growls angrily. She stops in front of a pile of fox droppings. Poor Little Fox! He must be so scared. Quick! He must be found.

Mother Fox begins to run again. She ignores the freshly turned soil in the meadow. She runs quickly along the trail of her little lost fox.

She stops sharply. This path has been trampled by humans, other animals, and machines. Little Fox has disappeared. Mother Fox is in despair. She breathes the air deeply into her nostrils. At last, in the fence, on a tuft of fur, she finds the scent of her little fox.

Quickly! Quickly!

Mother Fox keeps going, her snout to the ground. Suddenly, she raises her nose. A strong scent of birds is in the air, but there is also another scent — finer, more delicate. She sniffs again. Yes! A warm scent of frightened fox cub.